FIRE and SALT

Tarnelia
Matthews

Illustrated by
Rachel Moss

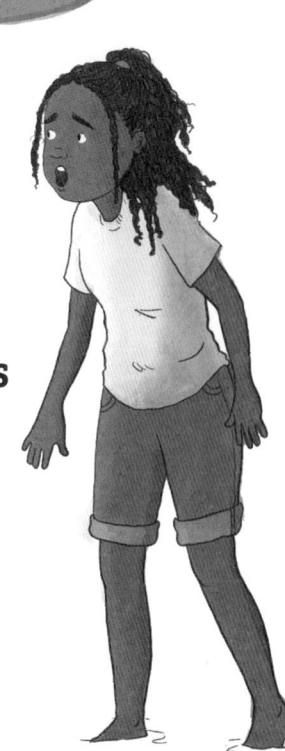

Collins

1 Cianne

I saw it here. *Right here.*

Sweet chirps of crickets and cicadas chorused around me, a reminder that even though no one was beside me, I wasn't alone. The evening air was thick, and my neck felt stiff from tilting my head back as I gazed up at the stars. I wanted to lie back on the damp grass, and stretched out my legs to do so, when I saw the orange streak blaze through the sky.

My heart jumped, excitement fluttering under my skin as my eyes locked on to the glowing orb, watching it slice through the darkness and disappear over the thick canopy of trees on the horizon.

It looked closer this time.

This was the third time this week that I'd spotted the orb. Thoughts raced through my mind, crashing

into each other. Was it a shooting star? Maybe a comet? I'd learnt about comets in school, and meteor showers; there was one called the Perseid meteor shower, which Mum let me stay up for last month. I fought sleep to watch the sparkling meteorites dash through the sky, but it was all worth it. Grandpops would have been proud; even though I fell asleep in Maths class the next morning and had to sit through a whole hour of detention, being lectured by Mr Maloney with the dusty moustache.

But this was nothing like that meteor shower. This streak was something else, something fierce. A bold, bright flaming ball, leaving a thick trail of fire in its wake; lighting up the sky as it snaked through. And it looked the same every single time.

If I could just get a little closer; maybe even get a picture.

I stared long and hard at the trees, waiting. Maybe I was secretly hoping some flames would emerge or the leaves themselves would begin to spark and glow that same orange blaze. I'd never seen anything like it before, but I kept seeing it, whatever it was.

And that is what I told Ramone the following evening. The same Ramone who now seemed more focused on the rock cake he'd bought as a snack, rather than the star-studded sky above us.

"You've been watching too many movies. You ain't seen no ghost," he said.

Ramone picked the currants out of the cake and piled them up on the dirt beside him. He used to save them for me when we were younger, but today he flicked them at my legs; little soggy bullets that the ants would feast on later. I wondered if he'd been listening to me at all.

"Ramone, I never said that I saw a ghost, I said that I saw a – a thing."

He scrunched up his face, and shot me a sideways glance, deep grooves settling between his sharp brows. His mouth was halfway between a smile and a frown, crumbs gathered in the corners.

"Cianne. You mean to tell me that you dragged me clear out here 'cause you believe you saw a UFO. Is that what you're really telling me?"

He flicked another currant; this time it hit my cheek.

I know he thinks I'm joking, playing another prank. I had half a mind to drag the cake out of his hand. "I'm not joking, Ramone."

"Suuure, Cianne."

"It's true! It was right over there." I jabbed my finger in the direction of the canopy where I'd watched the "thing" disappear. "It was this – it was like an orb."

Ramone stifled a giggle. "A what?"

"An orb! You know, like a ball thing, and it was glowing like fire – a fireball!" I sounded breathless trying to explain, my hands making shapes in an attempt to make my description clearer. It reminded me of the game charades that we used to play with Grandpops every Sunday after dinner.

"A fireball? Like the sun. You saw the sun," Ramone smirked.

This time, I really was about to drag the cake out of his hand. "Ramone, are you even listening? Not the sun. It was night-time, for goodness sake!"

"*It was night-time, for goodness sake.*" Ramone mimicked me in a whiny tone, waggling his finger at me, before flicking another currant.

I rolled my eyes so hard in my head, I'm sure they did a 360-degree turn. Ramone could be annoying at the best of times, as much as any older brother could be, but this evening he was truly exceeding himself.

I took a deep breath and tried again. "OK, look. The other night, I was here, and I saw the orb land over there; you know I know my stars, Ramone. Even in all my nights stargazing with Grandpops, I'd never seen anything like this."

Ramone looked up at me when I mentioned Grandpops. He looked like him: the same jaw, the same smooth dark skin. He even had the same deep dimple in his left cheek when he smiled. Right now, he wasn't smiling though. He was scanning my face the way he does when he's trying to sniff out a lie.

"So every night you've been out here, which makes three nights this week, Monday, Wednesday and Saturday, you saw this … orb." He gestured with his hands, his eyes on mine the whole time, searching for weakness.

I nodded and kept his steely gaze.

"But you don't have any real evidence, no picture, no video."

"No, it's too fast to catch and I never know when, or even if, it's coming."

He raised an eyebrow. "And so you brought me out here so that I can see it for myself?"

For some reason, I began to feel nervous. Ramone's mock detective interrogations were nothing new to me, but there was something about it this time that rattled me. This time I had something to prove. I took a steady breath before answering. "Yes."

"Even though you don't know if it's coming?" Ramone asked.

"Huh?" He was trying to catch me out.

A slow smirk crept up on Ramone's face. "Well, you just said that you never know when or even if it's coming, right?"

"Yeah but – "

"And so, doesn't that mean that maybe it isn't coming at all?" he said.

"Yes but – "

"So, we could be out here the whole night and see nothing, right?" Ramone reasoned.

He doesn't believe me. "Ramone, you won't even look!"

Ramone jerked his neck back and opened his eyes wide, making a deliberate show of looking. As deep as the night was, the whites of his eyes were bright, almost shiny, as they rolled left and right.

"There. I looked." He stood up and brushed off his khaki shorts, golden cake crumbs showering the grass. "I'm going inside, it's getting late and I ain't missing the football for this. It's a good thing the house has cable; can you imagine six weeks in Seabay with no Premier League?"

I turned away, frustration rising to my temples. It's fine. *It isn't.* He doesn't have to look to prove that I saw anything, anyway. *But I want him to.* I'll just take a picture or a video and then he'll see! Or I bet someone else will mention it and then he'll be the first one talking about how he saw it with his two eyes. *Typical.*

He'd only taken a few steps, his rubber soles crunching on the damp grass, when he stopped. "Cianne." His voice was different, hushed and low. It came out more like a low hiss than a whisper.

"What Ramone?"

"Cianne!"

I spun round, my braids slapping me across my cheek. "What?"

Ramone was standing dead still, poised, ready to take another step, but his foot hadn't quite met the ground.

My breath caught in my throat. I hadn't even eaten any cake, but my stomach was churning. I didn't realise I'd already stood up and made gentle barefoot steps towards Ramone, trying to see what had spooked him. I reached his side, one step behind.

"You don't see it?" he said.

Ramone's eyes were fixed on whatever it was he saw before him. I didn't know what it was that had transfixed my brother, but it didn't feel good. I needed to know.

"Ramone, what is it?" My throat was dry, my whisper caught in my breath.

"Right there, Cianne. Look!" He pursed his lips, nudging me to look in front of him.

I squinted hard, looking into the dark. I took a step closer. He gripped my arm, urging me back.

"You really don't see it?" His voice flickered, a tremble in his pleading. He squeezed my arm.

Although it felt impossible to do, I looked harder. I squinted till my eyes were sore, and I blinked to sharpen my focus. I took another step.

"Ramone, I don't see – "

"FIREBALL!" Ramone yelled, and yanked my arm back so hard I fell, my left knee grazing a rock in the grass. There was a hot buzzing under my skin and my heart was thudding in my ears as hard as it was hammering against my ribs.

It was Ramone's laughter that broke through the shock. He was on the ground, open palm slapping the grass, choking on his giggles; he could barely get his words out. "I didn't see anything either!" He started rolling again.

I scrambled to get off the ground, frantic to find something, anything. A rock, a shoe. *My shoe!* I grabbed my sandal and threw it at him. It missed and he laughed harder, his face contorted with the effort. "Ugh! You're such a fool Ramone. I can't even – "

I threw my other sandal. This time it connected with his shoulder. My hands were shaking so hard,

I'm surprised I could even grip the sandal to throw it. My heart was still hammering away at my ribs, skin prickling with heat and frustration. "You stay there laughing at me, Ramone."

My breath wasn't catching any more, instead it was rising like the heat under my skin. "You take everything for a joke. Everything!" I was shouting now, my voice quivering, along with my eyes, brimming with hot tears, which annoyed me even more. I blinked them back, furiously.

Ramone had caught his breath, his laughter now a contented little giggle. "Cianne."

I stalked past him, collecting my sandals. My arm was throbbing.

"Ciaaane, come on, you know that was funny," Ramone called after me.

I kept walking, leaving Ramone to joke by himself in the dark.

2 Ramone

Cianne sat silent as Aunty Jill placed a plate of sliced sweet bread on the table. Aunty Jill made the *best* coconut sweet bread, and she'd popped in with our cousin Sasha to drop off a freshly baked batch, whilst Mum popped out before the stores closed for the night.

I watched Cianne tracing a finger across her plate, gathering what was left of the soft crumbs. Sasha sat beside her, sipping a mug of hot cocoa, her beaded braids clanking against the mug as she watched the two of us intently, waiting for someone to speak. It wasn't unusual for Cianne to be quiet. She could spend hours daydreaming out of a window, but the solid scowl set on her face was new and it didn't go unnoticed.

"What's wrong, Cici? Yuh face set like thunder."

13

Aunty Jill held Cianne's chin and tilted her face to the light, as if the explanation for the scowl was hiding in it. Cianne remained tight-lipped, eyebrows furrowed, but she rolled her eyes in my direction to express her disdain.

Aunty Jill placed a hand on her hip and raised a brow. I busied myself with my plate, even though I'd long finished what was on it. I learnt in school that if you avoid eye contact, the teacher was less likely to ask you a question; it usually worked too – except Aunty Jill is no typical teacher – well, at least, not a school one. I could feel her watching me, and

I knew to expect her big dark eyes once I looked up, with that same look Mum gives us when one of us is in trouble.

Great. Now I'll have to explain.

I paused. Technically, I was just playing around. I didn't even know why Cianne was so upset; I just wasn't silly enough to fall for her prank like she did mine. In fact, the more I thought about it, the more I realised that if anyone should be annoyed, it should be me.

"Cianne tried to prank me, and it failed, and now she's being a baby about it."

Cianne's eyes darted over to me, her mouth already open in protest. "Aunty Jill, he's lying!"

"If I'm lying then what are you doing, Cianne?" I said.

Sasha's eyes darted back and forth as she tried to bury a smirk in her cup of cocoa. She was enjoying this.

"What foolishness." Aunty Jill shook her head.

I could tell she was irritated by our behaviour. "You're both here arguing over pranks?"

"Mine wasn't a prank!" Cianne hit the table, making the crumbs dance on her plate. She looked surprised by her own outburst; we all were.

Aunty Jill pursed her lips. "Hm, you're not in London now, child, yuh hear?" Her fingers waggled at Cianne with each word. "Here in Seabay, children treat adults with respect, not backchat. I'm sure your mother has told you plenty of times."

As though she were summoned, Mum bustled in through the porch door, hands laden with big branches of Spanish lime, her forehead beaded with sweat.

Aunty Jill sniffed and turned towards me, her hands on her hips, and continued her scolding without missing a beat. "When I was your age, you think I had time for pranks? I had to climb the tree for breadfruit and pull up yam, before I even left for school! You overseas children with all this city life don't know nothing about hard work, but you wanna get vexed over fool-fool pranks. You want something to do? How about some chores? All of this social media. Face yuh books!" She kissed her teeth in annoyance and headed to the sink, pulling a Spanish lime from the stem.

Sasha sniggered. She was used to her mother's tellings-off and for once wasn't on the receiving end of them, but I could feel the heat of embarrassment rising up my cheeks.

Since Grandpops's funeral, everyone had been *different* towards us. Extra nice and extra careful. Summer holidays in Seabay were usually bright, boisterous and fun. We looked forward to them every year, escaping the concrete jungle of London to stay with Grandpops in the lush, sandy bays of Maquba. Mum called it our home away from home, and everyone would gather there for delicious Sunday dinners or to watch the cricket championships, cheering along together at the score or shouting at the TV. But this time, it felt heavy and bleak. The house felt empty without Grandpops in it.

Mum often let us stay up really late and sit out in the yard whilst family arrived, bringing fragrant dishes of curries and platters of fried fish and fritters; but it wasn't fun. It just wasn't the same without him there to enjoy it with us.

There'd been no room or energy for scolding about disagreements between Cianne and me. That prank felt like the first time I'd properly laughed in ages! It almost felt good to be bickering with her again. It felt *normal*.

Mum shook her head. "You two over here stressing your Aunty Jillian, huh?" She stood up beside Cianne's chair and stretched her slender arm around her shoulders. "Pops always did say when the place is too quiet, something's wrong."

She faced me with a faraway look in her eyes and smiled as she spoke. "You know, you don't just have his dimples; you're stubborn like him too!"

Aunty Jill chuckled gently in agreement.

I wish I was *more* like Grandpops; he always knew what to say, how to make Mum smile even when she was angry. The memory of him felt warm, but I couldn't stop the sinking feeling whenever anyone mentioned his name, and I hated to see the glossy look in Mum's eyes that kept creeping in, moments before tears would tumble down her cheeks.

I looked away to stop my own from falling.

"Mum, can Sasha stay the weekend?" Cianne piped up, breaking the silence.

I groaned inwardly. *Great*. One was irritating enough, but Cianne and Sasha combined were double the trouble.

"Well, provided your Aunty Jill and Sasha don't have any plans," Mum replied.

Aunty Jill pursed her lips, rolling the Spanish lime skin between her fingers. "No misbehaving!" she said.

"Yes, Aunty Jill," Cianne said. Sasha nodded solemnly.

"I mean it!" She raised a finger along with a warning brow.

"Promise, Mama!" Sasha grinned.

3 Cianne

Sasha hadn't even been in the bedroom for five minutes and she was already going through my things.

"Ooo, I like this one," she crooned, holding up a printed T-shirt dress. "We should do a clothes haul for my online channel! London fashion meets Seabay style!"

"Sash, we've no time for fashion, right now." I cut her off abruptly, my tone serious.

She peered over her glasses at me, confused and a little concerned. I knew that came off a little dramatic, but I figured we should get down to business, especially since Ramone was being no help. For all I knew, the fireball could show up again tonight!

"OK, so ... what's going on?" She leant back

on my bed, watching me curiously, twirling a braid between her fingers.

"Sasha, I saw something outside the other night."

"Like what?" she asked.

"Something like – I don't know."

Sasha rolled her eyes. "Cici, you must know, if you saw it!"

"Well, yeah, I saw it, but I don't know exactly what it was I saw."

Sasha looked irritated. "Describe it to me? Was it a bird? A dragon? UFO?"

"Maybeee – "

Sasha sat bolt upright, her beads fiercely clacking against each other.

"Are you being serious? Because I was watching a documentary the other night and I *definitely* think there are some aliens in Seabay."

"You do?" My mind started wondering again. I didn't really think much about aliens actually existing, but Sasha may have a point.

"Of course! Just look at Ramone. That's an alien if I ever did see one." She burst out laughing at her own joke, clapping her hands with glee at the insult my brother wasn't even present to hear. Ramone and Sasha were *always* joking each other.

"Sasha, I'm serious! I saw something. It was flying through the air on fire. I'm not sure where it landed, but I saw it, and not just one time either."

Sasha straightened up and adjusted her glasses, watching me closely. "Is this what you were upset about earlier – with Ramone?"

I nodded, still annoyed by my brother's behaviour.

"He really did get to you, eh? I jumped when you banged the table. I thought Mama was gonna hit the roof!" She paused. "Well, Ramone might not want to hear, but I'm all ears, cuz!"

I gave her the warmest grin. I knew I could count on her to hear me out. Even though we lived oceans apart, Sasha and I were so similar.

She promised that when she finished high school, she'd come to study in London. She loved the hustle and bustle of what Aunty Jill called "the city life". Meanwhile, I've always preferred the slow, laid-back vibes of Seabay, with its white sand beaches and soothing ocean. Grandpops called it paradise and he was right!

I thought about my last sighting of the fireball, telling Sasha exactly what I saw.

She listened intently, her eyebrows wiggling as she thought.

Finally, she spoke. "So ... you don't *think* it was a comet, but you don't *know* if it was a comet."

I nodded.

"Do you think I'm imagining things?" I ask.

"Nope." Sasha grabbed the notepad and pen from my bedside table. "But I do think we need a plan. Here!" She shoved them towards me and headed over to the large bay window overlooking the yard.

"What am I doing with these?" I asked, confused. I was trying to keep up with her train of thought.

"We'll need a timeline. When I was watching the Eerie Encounters series on TV, they said the best way to document an alien invasion is to make a timeline so we can track the order of events."

"Wait, what? An alien invasion?" I spluttered.

Sasha flicked the locks down on the window. "Yes. A glowing orb thing crash landing? Sounds like aliens to me!"

I raised an eyebrow. "Sash, I don't think – "

"Don't think what? That UFOs can land in Seabay?" she huffed, fogging up her glasses as she pulled on the stiff wooden window frame. "Come on, these aliens ain't gonna take pictures of themselves!"

Sasha took no time climbing out of the window onto the flat roof below, extending her arm to pull me down beside her.

"It's fine, the roof will hold," she said, as I gingerly stepped down. "I've been out here lots of times. Grandpops used to say it was the best spot to see Orion's Belt."

She was right; the garage roof *was* the perfect spot to see the star-studded sky over Seabay. The light from the moon gave the treetops a cool glow, highlighting a breathtaking view of the town.

Sasha crouched down and gestured for the notepad and pencil I was still clutching. Tearing out a page, she placed it in front of her and started scribbling. I knelt beside her to get a closer look as I watched her scan the space around her, drawing various squiggles on the page, which I eventually recognised were the makings of a map.

"We're here." She prodded at the circle in the centre. "Now, I need you to show me where you saw it."

I stood up and looked around, taking in the shadowy outlines of the local town hall, the Seabay shopping mall, Mr Eric's farm and Uncle Desmond's warehouse supply store.

I peered out. "There! I think – " I point to a spot just beyond the town hall beside a gathering of jackfruit trees.

"Well, we'd better get comfy; it's just gone sunset, it could be a long night." Sasha yawned.

"Sasha, we can't stay out here all night! Mum would never allow it."

Sasha rolled her eyes. "Well, she won't find out! D'you want my help or not?" She pulled her phone out of her pocket and propped it up, facing the evening sky.

I looked out towards the town hall and listened to the crickets singing their chorus. Anything could be out there, things we don't even know. What if there really are aliens, here, in Seabay? The island of Maquba was only small and Seabay was even smaller. What would they want *here*? My thoughts were interrupted by a faint rustling below. I looked down. *Probably monkeys,* I thought.

I stepped back to join Sasha, and then I heard it again, louder this time. Sasha leapt up beside me, scanning the bushes below. I reached for the phone to put the torch on.

"Don't!" Sasha hissed, tugging my arm. "You'll startle it."

Startle what? I stepped back and looked behind me, nervous.

Mum's just downstairs, there's no need to be scared, I reminded myself. *We're safe here!* But out there, in the darkness of the bushes, there was no telling. Grandpops used to tell us all kinds of tales about creepy creatures around Maquba Island, and Mum always warned him that he'd give us nightmares.

He'd wink and say, "*Better to know than to find out*." But right now, I wasn't sure if I wanted to know at all. My skin prickled at the thought of finding out.

"Look, there!" Sasha whispered, urgency creeping in her voice as she pointed towards a cool glow bouncing between wide, shiny leaves.

We knelt down, close to the edge of the roof,

trying to get a closer look; Sasha's breath was raspy in her throat as she leant further forwards.

It made me nervous watching her beaded plaits dangling over the roof's edge, so I grabbed onto her legs, pinning her so she wouldn't fall.

"Ow!" her voice rang out. She clamped her hand over her mouth as we both froze, straining to hear.

The rustling froze with us. I couldn't bear the suspense or the silence that came with it; if my stomach twisted in knots any tighter, I was sure I'd be sick! I decided to head inside, so I tugged on Sasha's leg but I wasn't quick enough.

At that exact moment, Sasha screamed and recoiled backwards. I gasped as a bright glow from the bushes illuminated her face, lighting up the space around her like a halo. I grabbed her as we made a dash for the window, hearts racing. We scrambled through it, tangling ourselves up in the curtain as we bolted back into the room.

Almost simultaneously, Mum came bursting through the door, concern drawn across her face. "What's going on up here?"

4 Ramone

I rummaged around the kitchen, my stomach rumbling at the sight of Mum's baked chicken leftovers sitting on the stove. Football always gave me an appetite and, after having a kick about with the local boys, I was beyond hungry. I should have made my way back ages ago; Mum had warned me not to be out past sundown, but it was hard to resist exploring the place on the way home; besides, the main road was blocked off.

I'd sat down at the mouth of a salt cave, one of many in Maquba, listening to the rhythm of the tide drift in and out. The salt glowed, sparkling like crystals under the remaining sunlight, taking on the colours of the sunset, a collage of red and orange that spread across the sky as the sun disappeared along the water's edge.

Grandpops used to take a handful of salt and sprinkle it in his pocket, saying it was good luck. We always thought it was strange; there was plenty of salt at home. But he'd just chuckle. "This ain't for eating," he'd say. "It's special … *Seabay's secret*," he'd whisper, with a wink.

That evening, I'd grabbed a handful and shoved it in the pocket of my shorts. I'd watched the local fishing boats bob against the waves, allowing my memories to wash over me like a flood, remembering last summer when we went fishing.

"Give a man a fish and you feed him for a day. Teach a man to fish and you feed him for a lifetime."

His words had echoed in my head and lingered in my chest. I didn't try to fight my tears and let them fall onto the damp sand where the warm seawater swept them away. *I wish he was here.*

It wasn't too late past sundown; I'd taken a couple of back routes through the bush to cut time. *Meh*, I shrugged, helping myself to a chicken drumstick. I'm sure Mum wouldn't mind that I was a *little* late.

I heard footsteps heading down the stairs as Mum entered the kitchen, with Cianne and Sasha in tow. Cianne and Sasha looked shaken and a bit spooked.

"What happened to you two? Looks like you've seen a ghost," I chuckled.

Cianne's eyes darted over to Sasha, who looked like she needed to sit down.

"Hmm, something like that," muttered Mum, putting the kettle on. "Some talk about aliens in the bushes?" She raised her eyebrows at me, ruffling my hair.

I rolled my eyes. *Not this again.*

"Fireballs and now *aliens*?" I leant towards Cianne and Sasha, lowering my voice so that Mum wouldn't hear over the bubbling kettle. "So, is that why you were up on the roof?"

Sasha gasped. "But how did you – " she whispered, pulling me into the living room to make sure Mum was out of earshot; Cianne followed closely behind.

Cianne narrowed her eyes at me, realisation creeping across her face. "It wasn't an alien." She pointed at me. "It was him. Wasn't it *Ramone*?" Her words fired out like hot little jabs.

Sasha gasped again. "No waaay. Another prank?" She paused and considered for a moment. "Hm! It was pretty good, I can't lie."

"Sasha!" Cianne nudged her in the ribs, clearly frustrated.

I shook my head. If I ever told Mum that I saw Sasha leaning over the edge of the roof with Cianne right beside her, she'd probably lock all the windows in the house, let alone if Aunty Jill found out.

"It wasn't another *prank*, Sash-eurgh, I was on my way back from football and cut through the back roads. It was dark so I was using my phone torch, and what did I see? The two of you dangling over the roof. What were you even *doing* up there?" I was genuinely curious.

Sasha opened her mouth before Cianne got the chance.

"Aliens," she said matter-of-factly. She flopped onto the sofa. "Aliens are in Seabay, and Cianne and

I are going to find them."

I almost burst out laughing.

"I mean, we don't actually *know* if there are aliens – " Cianne mumbled, shrugging her shoulders.

"No, that's true," quipped Sasha, "but that's why we had to set up our own surveillance!"

I looked at Sasha quizzically. "And you planned to do that on the roof? In the dark?" I asked, baffled. I was used to Sasha doing foolish things, but this felt like a bit of a reach, even for her.

"Think about it, Ramone. Cianne sees a fireball land in some trees after dark. We go to the roof with a camera and wait. We're bound to catch it on – " She jumped up, patting her pockets. "My phone!"

She darted about, panicking; we all knew Sasha losing her phone would be the end of her world, and Aunty Jill had already warned that if she lost it, she wouldn't be getting another one.

"It's got to be here somewhere!" she whined.

"Ha, maybe you dropped it hanging off the roof," I joked.

Cianne shot me a look of annoyance.

"It's probably still *on* the roof," she suggested. No sooner had she said this, than Sasha went bounding up the stairs with Cianne close behind.

"Stop di running!" Mum shouted, emerging from the kitchen. "I don't know what has got into those two." She looked at me. "Or you. You think I didn't realise it was dark when you came in this evening, hm?"

I dropped my head, scrambling for an excuse. "Well, the main road was blocked, Mum. People said there was a fire. So I had to go the long way."

Mum rested her hand on my face, watching my eyes. "A fire, hmm? Listen, I know di summer has been rough, but please, between Cianne convincing herself of aliens and you wandering in late running from bushfire, I'm not sure it'll take much longer till my hair turns completely grey. When I say before sundown, I mean it. And if there's an emergency, you know to call me. Seabay may be more peaceful than London, but I still need you two to be safe, OK? Look out for one another!"

I nodded and gave her a small squeeze. I could see how exhausted she was; her eyes were puffy, though I couldn't tell if it was from tiredness or crying. Sometimes, I'd hear her in the bathroom or catch her brushing away tears while she was preparing dinner. She'd blame onions, but we knew it was Grandpops.

I'd have to step up. I didn't want her worrying about Cianne and me too. I headed up to Cianne's room, only to find her and Sasha hunched over the phone.

"So? Did you get a video of the aliens?" I mocked, wading in and grabbing the phone from Sasha's grip. "Next you'll be saying aliens caused that fire people were talking about on my way home."

"Hey!" she snapped, attempting to snatch it back. "We don't know yet, we didn't realise it was still recording; there's at least 20 minutes of footage to go through."

I looked at the screen and scanned through the video, waiting for some action, but there was nothing but the night sky. *Just as I thought.*

I stuffed the phone in my pocket. "Well, you won't be doing that tonight. Maybe I'll check it out for myself."

"Give me back my phone, Ramone, you can't take it!" Sasha shouted.

"Watch me. Oh, and stay off the roof. Mum's got enough on her plate without you two screaming. Anyone would think you saw a duppy."

"Ugh! You're so … ugh!" Sasha huffed, wrinkling her nose like she caught a bad smell.

I looked at Cianne and pointed at the window. "If Mum catches you again – "

She nodded reluctantly. She didn't want to stress Mum out any more than I did. But she had a look in her eye; that defiant spark when she gets a bee in her bonnet, and I had the feeling she wasn't going to stop until it stung. The wise words of Grandpops crept into my thoughts again: "*Those who don't hear must feel.*" *Hmm.* Grandpops was always right.

5 Cianne

Ramone's words rang in my head: "*Anyone would think you saw a duppy*" ... First aliens and now *ghosts*?

Between that and Sasha's snoring, I struggled to get to sleep. When I finally *did* doze off, it was a blur of smoke, fire and monsters, as if every spooky story that Grandpops had ever told us decided to come alive in my dreams.

I woke up with a start, my mind racing and my nightshirt damp with sweat. It didn't help that I had Sasha's elbow prodding my side, as she sprawled out beside me fast asleep. The room was dappled in golden orbs as the sunrise bloomed through the curtains. Slipping out from under the sheet, I headed to the window, careful not to wake her.

It really was beautiful here: the palm trees, the sea sparkling along the horizon. I opened the window and climbed outside, feeling the breeze against my clammy skin.

I tried to shake the night's dreams from my mind, but I was on edge. *Aliens, fireballs, duppies.* I shuddered and focused on a little hummingbird, fluttering around the branches of a breadfruit tree, its electric blue feathers rippling in the dawn light. *I can see why Grandpops liked it up here,* I thought, getting lost in the dainty bird's movements. Then I spotted something in the distance, creeping upwards into the sky.

Mist? The morning dew was heavy and sometimes gave the appearance of fog rising, but this was different. It was thicker, heavier, grey smoke tinged with a red hue as it snaked up through the trees and lingered in the sky. *How strange.* My thoughts began to race. Maybe there was a BBQ? A bonfire? Sometimes, they light them on the beaches at night where the locals hang out. *But it's six o'clock in the morning!* Finally, my mind landed on the one thought that made butterflies flap furiously in my stomach.

The fireball.

It had to be! Except, this time, I wasn't feeling as excited as I was when I last saw it.

This time, I felt a sickening knot twist in my stomach as one particular figure from my dreams last night lingered in my mind. I could smell the smoke, and I felt the heat as it emerged from a smouldering crater in the ground, its eyes a blazing amber. I shook my head to release the thought, but my mind didn't want to let it go.

I jolted as I heard the rusted squeak of the window behind me and turned around so fast, I felt giddy. *Thank goodness, Sasha's awake.* Only, Sasha wasn't on the roof or by the window. I quickly walked back to find Sasha where I left her, sound asleep in bed, snoring softly, a beaded braid hanging out of the front of her silk bonnet.

Even the peaceful glow of the sunrise couldn't soothe the eerie sensation that made the hairs on my arms stand up. I quickly climbed through the window and back into the room, forcing the window closed with such speed that its rusted hinges let out a pitchy cry.

I winced and pulled the curtains shut, not wanting to taunt my mind any more with smoke monsters, and climbed back into bed, pulling the sheet up over my eyes.

Think of Grandpops, think of last summer, think of coconut slices and ice cream. I flicked through each happy thought in my mind like pages in a magazine, the way Mum told me to when I felt scared about something, until eventually I drifted back to sleep.

I woke up to Sasha shaking me. I sat up and rubbed my eyes, confused, as Sasha shoved something in my face.

"Cici, look!"

"Wh – what's happening?" My eyes focused. "Oh, Ramone gave you your phone back," I yawned, stretching out.

"No," Sasha scoffed with a satisfied smirk. "I took my phone back while he was still asleep."

She handed me the phone, jabbing her finger at the screen. "Do you see that?" she asked.

I squinted as she replayed the video.

"There!" She screenshotted the image of what looked like a blur of light. A blur of orange light streaming through the clouds and disappearing into the trees.

"Zoom in on it," I asked, squinting harder, wanting to be sure.

Fireball!

"I guess we missed it because of Ramone or whatever," Sasha said, "but it looks like your fireball to me! Didn't Ramone mention something about a fire on the road?"

She was right; I'd completely forgotten about that, too distracted by my horrid dreams.

"Sasha, can you make out where this is? Like, what direction the phone was facing?" I asked, thoughts whirring.

Sasha pushed her glasses up her nose. "Of course. It looks like it's right by Mr Eric's farm."

I wonder if this has anything to do with the smoke? I gulped, nervous to proceed. "Sash, do you remember the story Grandpops used to tell us, about the fire lady?"

Sasha tilted her head in thought, her satin bonnet threatening to slide off. "Oh! The old witch that tricks people with shapeshifting – what was her name again – " She clicked her fingers. "The Ember Witch!"

I nodded as she continued.

"And she travels through the air by – " Her voice trailed off as she looked at me, eyes widening.

"Fireball."

6 Ramone

I woke up to the smell of sweet plantain, and stretched out, the sun beaming over the bed as daylight greeted Seabay in full force. I could hear the clanking of crockery downstairs amongst the gentle murmuring of voices; no doubt the mosquitoes Sasha and Cianne were up, talking their usual nonsense.

I shook my head. After all their racket yesterday, playing detective, I foolishly attempted watching the video on Sasha's phone last night; only to start drifting off in the first five minutes. *Thinking of which …*

I checked the nightstand where I'd left it. *Gone. Typical Sasha.* I jumped out of bed and headed down to breakfast, my stomach growling with hunger.

Cianne and Sasha were sitting at the table, scooping up saltfish with fried breadfruit and dumplings, whilst Mum sipped her coffee and flicked through the paper; the radio was  broadcasting the news in the background. I smiled. Grandpops would always make us listen to the news.

"It's important to know what's going on in the world," he'd say, peering over his glasses with a stern look.

Sasha looked up at me with a smug grin and placed a protective hand over her phone.

I pulled a face. She was lucky I hadn't hidden it.

"Morning, Mum." I kissed her on the cheek and helped myself to a piece of plantain.

"Good morning, darling," she smiled, pointing to a mug of tea. "Here, drink up before it cools."

"Aunty," mumbled Sasha, through mouthfuls of dumpling. "Can Cianne and I visit Uncle Des at the warehouse today? He says he has treats for us. It's not far and we'll stick to the road."

"Well, if Des isn't too busy without you girls running around him. I'll give him a quick call."

"No, Aunty, no need," Sasha interjected quickly, her eyes darting between Mum and Cianne. "I spoke to him, and he said it was OK! He told me to come for lunch time. You can check if you like, but he's usually busy in the mornings with deliveries."

I noticed Cianne shift in her seat, eyes fixed on her plate, the way she does when she's trying to avoid something. *Or when she's caught in a lie.*

Mum looked at Sasha carefully. "Hmm, I don't want you wandering out by yourselves. I have someone coming by today, so Ramone is going with you."

I almost choked on my dumpling.

Mum shot me a look before I could even protest. I *knew* I'd get lumbered with these two!

Sasha and Cianne attempted to pipe up; Sasha

whining loudest. "But Aunty, I *live* in Seabay. I know it like the back of my hand!"

"Yes, but I'd much rather you all go together. Safety in numbers; you all have to look out for each other!"

I nodded and Mum squeezed my shoulders.

Sasha couldn't wait to get going; I'd barely stepped out of the shower before she started complaining that I was taking too long.

Cianne on the other hand was still quiet. She had a faraway look in her eyes, as though her mind was ticking in a different zone, and she nibbled on her fingers, something she always does when she's nervous.

We set out, the late morning sun beating down on our backs. I couldn't wait to get to Uncle Des's warehouse to grab a cold pineapple punch. Cianne and I fanned ourselves, beads of sweat dripping down our faces, as Sasha strolled along comfortably, unaffected by her hometown's fiery climate.

"This way." Sasha pointed down a dusty gravel path, away from the smooth concrete that led

us past the main road to the warehouse.

I hesitated as she walked up ahead. Cianne lagged behind, just a few steps in front of me. I figured I could take the opportunity to talk to her; I could tell something was up.

"What's up with you?" I nudged her with my elbow.

"Not like you're gonna listen, anyway," she muttered, shrugging.

"Well, I'm listening now," I offered. I stopped for a breather, sweat dabbling my top lip.

Up ahead, I could hear Sasha yelling for us to

come on, but the sun was so fierce that Cianne and I had to slow down.

"Do you remember when Grandpops used to tell us scary stories, about duppies and stuff," Cianne asked, breathless.

"Yeaaah, like the Rolling Calf and stuff?"

My mind pulled up memories of Grandpops sharing stories of the fiery ghost bull that would drag a heavy, rusted chain around its neck, through the streets.

She nodded. "Yes, but d'you remember the one about the Ember Witch?"

I nodded slowly. *This is what was bothering her?*

I remember clearly: Cianne turning all the lights on at night, too spooked to get to sleep. Grandpops told the best stories; he always made them feel real. Sometimes *too* real. But Mum always reminded us that they're *just* stories. No different to Cinderella or Hansel and Gretel.

We began to walk again, Sasha growing smaller in the distance as she strode on, tired of waiting around for us.

"Do you think any of them are real?" she asked, as though she could hear my thoughts.

I laughed. "Cianne, I think all this alien and fire stuff has got you spooked. You *really* believe there's a shapeshifting fire witch putting people to sleep in Seabay? Next, you're going to tell me you saw that trickster Bredda Anansi."

Cianne sighed. "Yeah, but Grandpops – "

"Isn't here. And neither is the Ember Witch," I said, shutting down her spooky suspicions.

I swallowed painfully hearing the words leave my lips, as Cianne winced, her face downcast at the unnecessary reminder of Grandpops's absence.

She nibbled at her fingers, voice quiet. "Maybe it's like you said, probably a comet – right?"

I opened my mouth to agree but another sound launched into the air before I could get a chance.

Sasha screaming.

7 Cianne

I sprinted up the dust gravel path, hot on Ramone's heels to get to Sasha, my insides buzzing with panic.

Ramone reached her first. He put his hands on her shoulders and demanded to know what was wrong. The smell of smoke was thick in the air, leaving a bitter taste at the back of my throat. Sasha was sweating now, as she flapped her arms about.

"There – " she shuddered.

She pointed over to a wooden market stall: cowrie jewellery and wood carved trinkets hung from its splintered beams. A radio playing tinny calypso tunes balanced on a table draped with a long black sheet and decorated with souvenirs: scented candles, fabric fans and beaded earrings. A small plastic chair was placed behind it, but no stallholder was in sight.

My breath hitched in my throat when I followed the direction of Sasha's finger. There was a thin red river snaking its way down the path from underneath the cloaked table, pooling on the ground and darkening the dusty gravel before us.

I gulped. "Is – is that *blood*?" I asked, wincing.

Ramone grimaced and hesitantly stepped forwards.

"Be careful!" I hissed, reaching out to pull him back, my nerves rattling.

He crept towards the cloaked table and peeked around it, the radio hissing static in his presence. Then he paused, squinting.

"Ramone, let's just g—" I began to plead.

He ignored me and bent down, disappearing behind the stall for what felt like hours. I held my breath till he emerged, carrying a cooler piled with colourful bottles of fruit juice. He placed the cooler down and squatted, quickly standing to brandish an empty bottle, the remnants of its ruby red contents still swirling at the bottom.

"Just sorrel juice," he grinned. "Someone must have dropped it."

Sasha exhaled a relieved whistle, but her eyebrows were still furrowed. "Something's off," she said quietly. "I can feel it."

Ramone nudged her. "Oh, come on, you scared of some juice, Sash?" he teased.

I almost admired Ramone's ability to make light of things; at least one of us wasn't scared.

Sasha was right though. It *was* strange. What

was a stall doing here, abandoned at the peak of midday with no one there, just a rusty old radio? What if someone stole something? I wandered around the stall, smoke tickling my nose, whilst Ramone helped himself to a pineapple juice from the cooler.

"You'd better put that back," I warned.

Ramone rolled his eyes. "Well, it's not like there's anyone here to stop me," he scoffed.

"Exactly!" retorted Sasha. "There is *no one here*."

The tinny radio crackled, its music jarring and staggered.

"Look!" Sasha picked up an open tin, revealing coins and tattered notes inside.

Who would leave their money behind too? I thought.

Ramone sniffed, swirling the juice. "OK, that *is* a bit strange. But maybe they've gone for lunch? I've been smelling that smoke since we set out this way; there must be a jerk chicken stall round here somewhere – " He sat down on the step, swigging from the bottle, beads of sweat tracing his jaw.

Or maybe there was an emergency, and the person had to get away. Maybe we need to do the same … I shook the thought from my head, but my arms still had goosebumps, despite the sun beating down on us from the cloudless blue sky.

"I don't have a good feeling about this, Cici," Sasha shuddered, standing beside me. "The plan was to trick Ramone into going to Mr Eric's farm; I'd no idea we'd bump into all this on the way!"

Before breakfast, we'd decided to check out the suspected fireball location ourselves. There was no way Mum would have agreed to it, so Sasha's lie that we were going to Uncle Des's warehouse was the next best thing, and by the looks of things, for good reason. Something was up with Seabay. I could feel it in my bones, and I wished I didn't.

I tried to rationalise my thoughts, an attempt to overcome the creeping anxiety tying knots in my stomach. "Look, Ramone made a fair point – maybe the stallholder went to eat or had to run and get something."

Sasha rolled her eyes, pushing her glasses up her nose. "So, someone conveniently left their stall, money and goods behind on this road, to go and nyam food, eh? I don't know how they do things in London, but here in Seabay, we'd say that something fishy is going on." She leant forward and whispered, "Wouldn't surprise me if it was an alien abduction."

I was leaning against the wooden beam in thought, when I noticed something that made my stomach lurch. "Look." I gestured over into the bushes. Behind the stall, a grey ribbon was weaving its way upwards into the sky. *Smoke.*

Ramone sniffed. "So I guess that's where the food stall is at. I could do with a likkle jerk chicken."

Sasha shook her head. "I don't think that's a jerk chicken smoke smell, Ramone," she muttered. She shot me a doubtful look, but Ramone caught it. Sometimes, I forgot how quick-witted he could be.

"Oh, *come on.* What do you think this is – fireball part two? Oh, I know – " He hunched over, stepping out into an awkward spindly walk, twisting

58

and waggling his fingers at us. "The aliens have landed – " He deepened his voice in a mock growl. "Maybe even … the *Ember Witch.*"

Sasha tutted in annoyance. "Must you really make a joke of everything, Ramone? It's not funny!" She placed a hand on her hip: a perfect replica of Aunty Jill.

"Oh, of course, it is!" he chuckled.

Maybe Ramone wasn't scared, but I couldn't shift the eerie feeling in my bones that had been stirring since early morning. I wanted to believe it wasn't real and laugh along with Ramone's nonsense, but I couldn't quite ignore the alarm bells jingling in my head.

"I'm hungry and I want to get some jerk chicken – you coming, or not?" He began to set off, casting a look over his shoulder, expecting us to follow.

"*Better to know than to find out.*" Grandpops's words rang out in my thoughts, like a delicate bell.

I guess we're about to find out.

8 Ramone

My stomach rumbled as I followed the dusty trail, anticipating the juicy barbequed meats that would be on offer. I glanced over my shoulder to see Sasha and Cianne close behind. In their defence, the abandoned stall was pretty strange, but old witches and aliens? *Pshhh, no way.*

I'd almost forgotten about the Ember Witch until Cianne mentioned it earlier. She unlocked a memory. Grandpops would burn rubbish in the old steel barrel outside and have us gather round it. Smoke danced in the air as he warned us of the witch's wicked ways.

"Stay wise and protect yuh energy. Tings are not always what they appear to be," he'd caution. His husky voice and sparkling eyes always kept us on our toes. We'd hold our breath, hanging

on to his every word as he spoke; his words flowing and rhyming like a song.

"Should she find your town, it might be too late.
She'll put yuh to sleep and yuh may never wake – !"

He'd slam the lid on the smouldering barrel with a bang, and laugh, a big, hearty sound that could lift the darkest of moods. Then he'd cradle us all close and remind us that no fire witch would ever find us, so long as he was around. I closed my eyes at the memory, a stiff ache pounding in my chest, knowing that he wasn't around any more.

He may not be here, but his memories are. His legacy is, I reminded myself. It's all I'd been hearing from relatives since the funeral. It didn't feel particularly comforting; I'd have much preferred him to speak to, to laugh with. If Grandpops was here to hear Cianne and Sasha, he'd be laughing and challenging me to a race to the jerk chicken stand. He'd be reminding them that there's nothing to fear. Just like I was doing now.

The smoke was stronger now, and my eyes had prickling tears in them. But as I searched the trail ahead, I saw nothing but deep green foliage – thick shrubbery with waxy leaves that reflected the sunlight, and cricket song singing out from beneath them. Even the trail became swallowed up by it.

Cianne and Sasha stood beside me as I fanned the air, scoping out the space ahead, flattening the tall grass.

Sasha nudged Cianne and whispered loud enough for me to hear. "See, no jerk chicken."

Determined, I continued on, heading further down the path, which began to wind down a hill.

I pushed through leaves and snapped branches until the ground levelled out and I was forced to stop. I blinked, confused, as my eyes settled on smouldering embers that had scorched a shallow crater into the earth in front of me. Branches were still alight, as fiery foliage contributed to the plume of smoke dancing above us.

Sasha gasped behind me.

Cianne's eyes grew wide at the sight "What on earth – "

… *happened here?!* I silently finished Cianne's question.

Cianne looked at me, expectantly, as though she was waiting for an explanation, but I couldn't give her one. I had no idea.

"Well, I guess your fireball theory was right, after all, Cici," quipped Sasha, looking around.

"Listen. I know this is strange, but I'm sure there's a logical explanation for this!" I reasoned.

Sasha turned round to face me. "So, what's

your explanation for *that*?" she hissed, pointing at something beyond the smouldering crater.

There, under the shade of a banana tree, was a bull. A large, black, muscled bull with a rope attached, the end of which looked singed and frayed from fire. Its eyes burnt a deep amber, as though the flickering orange of a flame was dancing behind the sockets. It lay still, immobilised, eyes fixed.

Cianne exhaled shakily, backing away, whilst Sasha appeared rooted to the spot.

"Is it dead?" Cianne whispered.

I knew better than to check or make any sudden movements. If that bull decided to charge us, we wouldn't stand a chance.

Sasha shook her head. "It's still breathing … I can see it." Her eyes remained fixed on the bull, and I could see the subtle rise and fall of its body, its silky coat dulled by a thin layer of ash.

I blinked hard to clear my vision. *Come on, Ramone, what would Grandpops do?* I took a deep

breath. "Sasha, back away slowly – " I gently reached forwards, my hand outstretched for her to hold on to.

She exhaled shakily, her nose whistling with each breath. "It's gonna get up … I can't," she trembled.

"You can!" I hissed. "You have to. Come *on*. I've got you."

She began to move, taking care where she placed her shaky footsteps, fearful that the branches crunching beneath our feet might alert the beast.

Cianne turned to look at me. "What if it sees us?"

"It won't." I tried to reassure her, completely unsure myself. The panic in her eyes told me she didn't quite believe me either. I stretched further. "Sasha, *come on!*"

The bull released a deep grunt and stirred. I held my breath and stood still, my body suspended in motion, but Sasha squealed. She ran, slipping on the leafy undergrowth. Her sandal gave way; the ankle strap snapped and sent her flying towards me. She hurtled into me, and we both crashed to the ground, my foot folding awkwardly underneath my weight. A sharp pain shot up my leg making my eyes water.

"Arghhh-mmmph!" Cianne clamped her hand over my mouth to stifle my yell, her eyes panicked and darting towards the bull, but it didn't move. It was as if it couldn't see or hear us.

Sasha scrambled, unscathed, towards us. She knelt over me and checked to see where I was hurt. I tried to stand, but my foot couldn't take the weight. I bit my fist to stop myself from crying, as Sasha nestled herself under the crook of my arm, offering support.

"My phone," I muttered, pulling it out of my pocket. I dialled Mum, squinting through sweat to see the screen, but the call wouldn't connect. *No signal.*

Sasha patted her pockets, helplessly. "I left mine at home."

"I'll get help," muttered Cianne.

"Help from *where*?" hissed Sasha. "We're not even on the main road. Ain't nobody round here. Even that stall was empty."

"I can manage." I spoke with gritted teeth, as I attempted to limp another step; my foot throbbed so hard, it felt like it had another pulse.

"You can't manage safely, Ramone. I think Cianne's right; one of us will have to get help."

"Maybe the stallholder will have come back," I suggested weakly, the pain swallowing my words.

Cianne looked at me and her face contorted with worry. "It's OK, Ramone, I'll go."

9 Cianne

I ran back up the verge, sweat beads trickling into my eyes. The fierce midday sun sizzled my skin as I stretched my arm up high, waving Ramone's phone about, desperate for a signal. My thoughts were speeding quicker than I could catch them: *the stall, the smoke, the fiery crater, the giant bull ...*

For once in my life, I really hoped Ramone was right, and that the mystery stallholder would be at the stall, full of lunch and ready to help. If not, then I wasn't sure where I'd head to. I wasn't sure how to get home or make it back into town from this area of Seabay; it was unfamiliar to me, and Sasha had been leading the way.

I glanced back over my shoulder and saw their figures behind me, hobbling towards the verge. It would take them a while to reach me, but at least they were making *some* progress. I kept running, kicking up dust with my sandals as I escaped the bushy undergrowth and made it back onto the gravel dirt path. I could faintly make out the tinny radio cranking its tunes from the wooden stall, and as I got closer, the figure of somebody standing beside it.

Thank goodness.

My heart leapt. Somebody must have seen the smoke! Or maybe the stallholder really did come back. I began to wave, slowing down a little to give way to the stitch tearing at my side. "Hey! Hello, *hello!*" my voice croaked, as I yelled for their attention, waving harder. I looked back behind me; Sasha and Ramone were gaining up the verge, albeit slowly.

Not long now.

The person began to walk towards me, and I squinted, trying to make out their features. The smell of smoke tickled my throat and made me cough. As the figure got closer, I realised it was a woman. Dark locks were piled high on top of her head, wrapped in a deep red cloth, and the loose cotton kaftan draping her slight frame was adorned with bright patterns.

She slowed down, her feet ashen and bare, distorted with dips and cracks, her face a smooth, deep brown that glowed against the sunlight. She fixed her deep-set eyes on mine. I tried to clear my throat before speaking again, the smell of smoke more potent than before.

"Hello, ma'am," I said. "Sorry to bother you, but thank goodness you're here. My brother hurt his foot and we need some help to get home, but there's no signal and there's … there's a bull, but we think it might be passed out or something, and there was a crater and a fire! Please, if you could help or if you have a signal, can I use your phone?"

I knew I was rambling, my words crashing into each other as I tried to get my thoughts in order. I waved Ramone's phone around and pointed down the verge, in an attempt to make sense.

The woman continued to stare at me, nodding slowly as she digested my words. She had a strange smirk twisting on her lips, which made me feel uneasy. She raised a hand with long, ink black, brittle nails that jutted out of gnarled and twisted fingers, just like the bark from an old tree Ramone and I used to swing on as kids. I gasped, hairs rising on my arms and the back of my neck, as I took in the sight before me.

It couldn't be …

Her eyes were glowing embers, with orange irises swirling like rings of molten lava as she began to smile, her face widening to reveal sharp, pointed teeth like little porcelain daggers. I staggered backwards, my legs heavy as lead weights. I wanted to run, I wanted to scream, but I couldn't make any sound; my mouth froze open in shock.

She began to chuckle, a deep rattle that rose out of her chest into a creaking pitchy laugh that hurt my ears and made me wince.

My feet felt rooted to the ground as I watched her take another step and point into the space behind me, her eyes ablaze.

Ramone and Sasha.

Ramone wouldn't be able to escape even if he wanted to; they had no idea the Ember Witch was here.

"Get … away!" I screamed, throwing Ramone's phone at her as hard as I could. It connected with a dull thud but did nothing to stop her tracks. My legs buckled as I shuffled back, trying to widen the space between us, my hands scrabbling at the dusty gravel, trying to find something, *anything* to throw.

I had to warn them. I had to stop her.

10 Ramone

An awful sound pierced the air, followed by Cianne's scream, that shook me to my bones.

Without missing a beat, Sasha took off, sprinting up the verge, her plaits flailing in the wind.

"Cianne!" I called out, willing my legs to move faster. My T-shirt was heavy with sweat, and I was already exhausted with my efforts. Despite the blazing sunshine on my back and the searing heat from my throbbing ankle, my skin was prickled with goosebumps from a chill that even the sun couldn't break. I *needed* to get to Cianne.

"Cianne!" I yelled again, biting through the pain as I gained speed, limping up the hill. "Sasha?" I shouted, my voice cracking with panic as I broke into a clumsy run, adrenaline masking the pain. I didn't dare look behind me; I was sure all the noise would have roused the bull, but I couldn't think about dealing with that now, not when my family was in trouble.

I finally made it to the dirt gravel path. Sasha was kneeling, trying to calm down a visibly shaken Cianne.

Cianne sat on the gravel, her eyes wide and glassy with tears; her hands trembled and she tried to catch her breath. Her tears spilt over when she saw me and she leapt from the ground, throwing her arms around me in a tight embrace, nearly sending me flying again.

"Are you OK? What happened to you? Who was here?" I pulled her away, inspecting her and the bushes around us, my fingers gripping her shoulders. "Was it another bull?"

She shook her head as she looked around, as though she was searching for something or *someone*.

"Cianne, what is it?" cried Sasha, shooting me a worried look.

"She – she was just here. Just here and – and then she was gone."

"*Who* was here, Cianne?" I said. I could feel myself getting impatient.

She shook her head and looked at me and then Sasha. I could sense she wanted to speak; her eyes were already speaking far louder than words, but she was hesitant.

Cianne took a deep breath. "Th – there was a woman. I thought maybe she was from that old stall – except – " She shuddered, wrapping her arms around herself. "She had these awful, long nails – like – her hands looked all, twisted up." Cianne grimaced, recalling the details. "Her nails were black and her feet were all crusty and – "

I looked at Sasha. She seemed as confused as me.

"She was wearing a dress – a lovely dress and her hair – " Cianne shook her head again, as if trying to shake the image from her head.

"OK, maybe she *was* the stallholder, after all!" Sasha suggested.

"Maybe," Cianne mumbled. "But – " she paused, her eyes darting around. "But – her eyes." Cianne's voice came out as a hoarse whisper, as though she didn't want to speak the words coming out of her mouth. She shuddered again, shaking her hands the way she does when she sees something she doesn't like, like a spider.

"Her eyes?" I repeated, waiting for her to finish.

She looked at me. "They weren't normal, Ramone – they were like the bull's, like fire."

I was confused. *How could that be?*

Sasha looked scared, the grooves between her eyes deeper than I'd ever seen.

"Well, what did she say? What did you say?" I asked.

Cianne took a breath. "Nothing. Well – not nothing – I asked for help and that's when she – " Her voice cracked, "She just laughed at me. She had horrible, jagged teeth and those eyes. That awful sound." She began shaking her head as though she was trying to dissolve the memory.

That horrible sound was laughter? I heard it. Sasha did too. It made my blood run cold.

Cianne looked at me with an expression I hadn't seen in some time. She was scared.

The sound of crunching gravel broke the tension, and Cianne jumped, startled. She heaved a sigh when she spotted Uncle Des's truck rolling down the path, and her fists unclenched.

Mum barely even let the truck roll to a stop before she jumped out of the passenger side, her face contorted with worry.

"What on *earth* are you all doing out here? What's going on?" Her arms flailed as she registered my lopsided stance, my left foot barely resting on the ground, Sasha's missing sandal and Cianne's tear-streaked face. She looked behind us, at the smoke from the mysterious burning crater, which was still snaking through the air, creating a dark cloud over the trees.

"I knew, I should have followed my spirit! I knew yuh all was up to something this morning – it's a good thing I called Des to check if you'd reached the warehouse safe. But not only had you not reached it, he didn't even know you were coming!" Her voice was raised now as she gave a pointed look at Sasha, whose head was bowed, embarrassment tingeing her cheeks. "If it wasn't for that smoke, we wouldn't have even looked this way. Goodness knows what could have happened to you!" She grabbed us together and gave us a frustrated squeeze. "How'd you all even end up out here?" she demanded.

We all looked down, no one wanting to be the first to speak.

Technically it *was* my fault. I was the one who wanted to prove a point and insisted on looking for jerk chicken. Guilt gnawed at my insides – the last thing I wanted to do was upset Mum, yet here she was, stressed and ranting – and for good reason too.

Sasha quietly piped up, to my surprise. "We were hungry, and thought the smoke might have been from a jerk pan."

Mum tutted. "Really, chil'ren? *Really?* All ah this for a hungry belly? You would think I never fed you! Good grief, what am I going to tell your mother now, hmm?" She fussed, one hand wiping Cianne's tears, her other arm around my waist, helping me hobble to the truck.

Uncle Des was trying to get a better look at the smoky view and tripped on an object on the floor – my phone.

He picked it up and brushed it off. "You ain't

gone be able to use dis for now, eh?"

I frowned as he handed it to me; its screen was smashed and splintered.

On the drive home, Uncle Des seemed troubled by the smoke. He scratched his shiny bald head in confusion, clearly puzzled by our rambling accounts, and he was even more baffled when we mentioned the disappearing woman, the bull and how I'd hurt my ankle.

"It's very strange," he mused. "I never hear of a such a thing in Seabay yet! Yuh all very lucky that bull never charged yuh. If it's anything like the ones on Mr Eric's farm, it would've run yuh down! I'll have to call him to check it out."

He chuckled, tapping the steering wheel. "I tell ya, if Grandpops was here, he would've sworn it was a rolling calf. You sure that fire-eye woman you say you saw wasn't di old Ember Witch?" He chuckled again, his round belly heaving against the steering wheel.

"None of those stories, please, Des," Mum

scolded him. "I think the children have had more than enough excitement for one day!" She turned and looked at us. "Pay him no mind, yuh hear?"

But we had heard, and I felt a stirring in my stomach that made me feel nervous. *They're just stories, remember. Silly old stories that Grandpops used to tell us.* But Cianne looked at me, her stare unwavering, as though she could feel the stirring in my belly too. As though she was pleading with me to pay attention.

"Sometimes the truth is stranger than fiction." I heard Grandpops's words echo in my thoughts. What if *this* time, fiction wasn't really fiction, after all?

11 Cianne

Night arrived quickly, and I shifted in bed, trying to get comfortable. I shivered even though the night air was warm and sticky, and I struggled to get those blazing eyes out of my head. It wouldn't be long until daybreak. I could tell from the shadows on the wall as light began to slowly creep through the curtain, but I wasn't sure I even had the energy to get up.

Sasha stirred next me and sighed, "I can't sleep either."

I rolled onto my back, closing my eyes. "I keep thinking about it … the bull, the woman. Where did she go? What does she *want*?"

I hadn't told her that I'd seen the woman point behind me at her and Ramone, her wicked laugh piercing the air.

I opened my eyes and turned to face Sasha. Her features were faint in the dim light. "I know it sounds silly, I do, but her eyes, that laugh – Ember Witch or not, that *thing* is not good. Not at all."

"Well, maybe it's time we finally figure out *exactly* what she is." Sasha jumped up and turned on the light, grabbing the notepad. She began scribbling, her brows furrowed in concentration. She pushed the notebook in my direction, triumphantly, as though she'd just completed a masterpiece.

There was a stick figure, with various arrows and descriptions pointing out of it.

I cracked a smile. It was the first time I'd felt like laughing for what seemed like years, even though it really wasn't funny.

Sasha tilted her head, observing her handiwork. "I'm sure it could do with a few adjustments, but *this* is our character profile.

And, judging by the evidence, it sounds like you were right all along, Cici. The Ember Witch is in Seabay."

At breakfast, Sasha and I plotted, thinking of ways in which we could learn more about our discovery. Creepy Seabayan tales were traditionally known in most Maquban households, but they were always told by elders. I'd never seen a book with any of those stories in them. When I asked Sasha if she knew of any old books, she giggled into her tea.

"Cianne, I know Seabay maybe ain't as tech savvy as London, but we *do* have the internet, you know."

Mum chuckled behind a newspaper, sipping her morning coffee. "You two *detectives* have had more than enough adventure, yuh hear? Look what happened to your brother. I had to mek up a bed downstairs so he could rest that foot of his!"

Ramone came hobbling into the kitchen, wincing as he sat down. He placed his foot on the chair opposite. "Mum said to keep it elevated," he shrugged, wiggling his toes.

Mum headed out of the room to make a call, and Ramone reached forwards for the morning paper. He reminded me of Grandpops – legs stretched, morning paper and a hot tea. I was allowing myself to drift in the memory, when Ramone jolted so suddenly he nearly rocked back on the chair.

"Have you seen this?" He spread the paper out on the table as Sasha began to read the article aloud, her fingers jabbing at the text.

Mysterious illness taking down Seabay cattle could be a threat to locals

Trance-like sleep phenomenon has scientists puzzled as it spreads throughout the Seabay area of Maquba. Bovine specialist Professor Mitchell reports that the cattle appear to be in a state of sleep paralysis, though their eyes are open. A key symptom is an unusual change of colour to their irises.

My eyes scanned the page quicker than my brain could register the words. I froze when I saw the picture. "That's her!" I said, breathless. "The Ember Witch."

88

My heart was racing. She had the same soft brown skin, the same dark locks piled up high. Only in this picture, her beaming smile was soft and dazzling, there were no razor-sharp fangs like I'd seen yesterday, and her brown eyes were nothing like the fiery rings that made my hair stand on end.

Ramone shook his head. "Can't be – it must be her twin. It says here that this woman, a local craft seller, has been in the hospital for the past week. They fear she's the first human casualty of this ... strange sleep illness." He exhaled, whistling through his nose. "Boy, if it's spreading from cattle to humans then who knows what that means for Seabay. That explains the bull yesterday!"

But this isn't some strange mystery illness, I thought.

I knew Ramone would rather believe that I saw this poor woman's estranged twin than believe that the Ember Witch is real, but this gave me all the evidence I needed. I just needed to stop her, before she stopped us all.

Out in the yard, Sasha and I mulled over the newspaper.

"How is it possible that the Ember Witch is the same woman in hospital?" she questioned, chewing on a juicy piece of sugar cane from the bowl of fruits Mum had prepared for us earlier.

"She isn't … well, I don't think she is," I paused, reaching for a mango slice. I wasn't particularly hungry; seeing that picture in the article had my stomach in knots, but it was a welcome distraction and chewing helped me think. "The story Grandpops always told us – remember? He said that she could transform, or something like that. What was the rhyme again?"

Sasha twirled a braid and began to hum, mumbling a slow melody to herself, a tune that was warm and familiar.

I closed my eyes and cast my mind back to Grandpops and his deep brown eyes sparkling like starlight as he spoke. It felt majestic, sitting beside him and hearing him reel off his stories so fluently, no matter how creepy they were. He captured everyone's attention – even Mum's and Aunty Jill's – he never forgot a detail or missed a rhyme, and when I asked how he made up such stories, he would wink and say, "Who said I made them up?"

Ramone hobbled out into the yard leaning on Grandpops's old cane that he'd found. I don't know how long he was watching us for, but I jumped as he cleared his throat, a slow deliberate rumbling, the same way Grandpops used to before he'd begin one of his tales.

"*And juss like a comet, she blaze through di sky,*
an wait in di bushes fuh a passer-by.
She'll change up her face and take on their form,
she'll put dem to sleep, cackling till di dawn.
With eyes blazing fire and teeth razor sharp,
she hides in plain sight and she creeps in di dark.
Don't be like a moth and get caught in her flame!
She feeds off yuh energy to fly again.
She'll trick yuh and mek you believe di untrue,
she greedy fuh power, she won't stop wid yuh!
So gather your salt, from di glow of the bay.
Gather your salt and mek haste, no delay.
Gather it up so you can dash it down,
at her feet, on her skin, till she bun to di ground."

He sighed triumphantly when he'd finished, his eyes sparkling with honour at having recited Grandpops's rhyme so fluently. I'm sure I'd have felt bittersweet pride, if the dawning of his words hadn't caused panic to prod at my heart. He must have noticed mine and Sasha's alarmed expressions too because, within seconds, the smile on his lips had vanished and was replaced with wide-eyed realisation.

Sasha broke the silence. "That last bit! About the salt."

"*From di glow of the bay –* " Ramone murmured, his thoughts travelling.

Sasha's eyes lit up "Yes! I think I know where that is – we all do. Where did Grandpops used to take us to watch the fishing boats?"

Ramone's knowing look matched my own as we nodded at each other with understanding.

The salt caves.

12 Ramone

I couldn't quite believe I was going along with this. I shook my head in disbelief at my own thoughts as I considered whether there could actually be truth to the Ember Witch story. A *story* – one that seemed to be playing out in live action *here*, in Seabay. Surely, it had to be a coincidence – there must be an explanation.

"But sometimes the truth is stranger than fiction." Grandpops's words once again rang in my head. I rubbed my forehead in frustration. I wondered what he'd make of all this. I wondered if *he* had ever encountered the Ember Witch.

Cianne paced the floor. "How will we trap her?" she asked. "It was only by chance that we saw her yesterday. There's no guarantee that she'll be back at the same place again."

"Yuh forgetting the story *again*?" Sasha cried, exasperated. "*She greedy fuh power*, Cianne! I can bet you she drained that horrid bull's energy before she set on the poor street seller too."

A light bulb flicked on in my head at Sasha's words; she was right! The cattle of Seabay all seemed to be affected; maybe they were an easy target, before she decided to move on to trickier subjects … people.

"The farm. There are plenty of cattle there; if she hasn't got to them already, maybe they're her next target!" I suggested.

Cianne looked at me and smiled. I felt bad for doubting her for so long, when all she wanted was for me to listen to her. *Really* listen to her. All this time, Mum was telling me we needed to look out for each other; meanwhile, all I did was poke fun and dismiss everything she and Sasha had said.

Mum had left me in charge whilst she went to help Uncle Des with the warehouse inventory.

"We'll be back by sundown and I have my phone.

No gallivanting, OK?" She'd gestured to Sasha and Cianne before heading out. They were now talking excitedly on the back porch.

"We don't have a choice, if we don't go to the salt caves now, it might be too late," Cianne said decidedly, her stubborn streak flaring up again.

I knew we had to do *something*, but the thought of Sasha and Cianne running into danger was a risk we shouldn't be taking.

"I don't want to stick around to see who's next. What if it's Mum or Aunty Jill?" Cianne protested.

"Or *you*!" I pointed out.

"Salt is her weakness! I'm sure the caves are the last place she'd be. Besides, we can easily make it back by sundown! It's a 15-minute walk, ten if we run. Come on, Ramone, *please*. *Trust me*," she pleaded.

I didn't hesitate with my answer. "No, Cianne. No way."

She threw her hands up in the air in frustration and stormed into the house, Sasha chasing behind.

Cianne had made a good point about the salt caves but, after yesterday, it felt way too risky. It was then I remembered. *My shorts' pocket!* I'd taken a handful of salt that day on my way home from football, before all of this began. I smiled. *Thanks, Grandpops.*

I walked to the laundry room and rifled through the hamper of dirty clothes until I found them, dipping my hand in the pocket. It was still gritty with coarse clumps of damp salt. *Perfect.* This has to be of *some* use, *surely?*

I gathered what I could, emptying the pocket into a dry T-shirt to show Sasha and Cianne. Maybe this would stop them from doing anything extreme. But I was too late. On the dining table, there was a roughly scrawled note in Cianne's handwriting: *Trust me.*

13 Cianne

We ran past some locals. Some of them stopped us to say hello, or scolded us for bustling past them, tutting about manners, as we breezed down the roads. With Sasha's phone and Mum's cotton shopping tote in hand, we raced on. I was checking people's faces as I went past for any signs of fiery eyes or jagged teeth. My heart leapt, seeing the feet of some of the locals, unsure whether they were that of the Ember Witch or my eyes playing tricks on me.

The sun was scorching, dazzling against the fluffy clouds, but thanks to Sasha's short-cuts, we made it, the sea-salt air whipping our faces as the rush of the waves sprayed us with fine mists of water.

The mouth of the cave looked like it was glowing, the crystals blinding in the sun as they reflected the light, enticing us to explore inside. There was no need, nor was it safe to. Grandpops always told us to stay at the mouth and go no further; there were stalagmites that could be dangerous.

I hadn't been back here since Grandpops died and the familiarity of him was almost overbearing. I quickly brushed away tears as we scooped up the sandy salt and threw it in the bag.

"That should be plenty," breathed Sasha. "It's only di one witch, right?"

I smiled and glanced at Sasha's phone. *No missed calls. Phew.*

I knew it was a bold move to sneak out and I only hoped that Ramone didn't snitch on me. But even if I *did* get in trouble, I was willing to take the punishment; I was doing it for *us*!

"We bossing it, eh?" Sasha teased, nudging me with an elbow as we speed-walked back, cutting down another side road. The sky began teasing a sunset, with hints of oranges and pinks beginning to creep into view. "I can't lie, Cici, I wasn't sure we'd be able to pull this off. If my mum found out, she'd never let me leave the house again!" Sasha giggled.

We laughed, as I felt a small sense of relief rise in my chest.

We had the salt, and we were almost home. I was about to prove to Ramone that I'm not just his little sister. I'm just as smart and able as he is! Besides, Mum and Grandpops always told me there was nothing I couldn't do if I put my mind to it. We walked up the path approaching the house, breathing heavily. Ramone ambled towards us.

Sasha and I looked at each other as I braced myself for an argument. *Here we go …* But as we got closer and he came into view, he wasn't angry at all; in fact, he looked perfectly calm. *Too calm …*

"Before you start, we're fine *and* we made it back before sundown like we said we would!" I stated, Sasha nodding with enthusiasm beside me. But he didn't respond, or slow down. He carried on taking stiff, measured footsteps towards us. It was then I realised: he wasn't limping. I looked down at my brother's feet.

"Ramone?"

Sasha wobbled as she nudged me, a whimper leaving her lips. "L-look!"

But I'd already seen.

My heart plunged as I looked up to see my brother's eyes ignite, his irises glowing like hot embers, the same molten orange stare that had

100

been haunting my thoughts. His dimpled cheeks rose to reveal a smile. *That* smile. A sinister row of sharpened teeth that made my blood run cold.

The Ember Witch. Goosebumps prickled my arms as I watched her, in the form of my brother, walking towards me.

I wanted to scream but my tongue became heavy in my mouth, almost as heavy as my legs that didn't seem to want to step backwards despite my brain's orders.

The Ember Witch's shrill laugh cut through the air like a hot knife, scrambling my thoughts, as her long brittle nails stretched out towards me.

"Cianne – no!" Sasha cried out, launching herself at the witch, who stood firm against her blows, cackling harder as though she was mocking Sasha's feeble attempts.

I gritted my teeth, willing myself to move, but it dawned on me that it wasn't my fear that had me frozen, it was her. The closer she got to me, the slower I became; her eyes growing more intense

with each step, pulling me into her fiery trance.

"*Don't be like a moth and get caught in her flame!*
She feeds off yuh energy to fly again."

The words rang out in my mind clear as day,
cutting through the chaos. *Her eyes were the flame!*

I clamped my eyes shut and mustered up all the
energy I could. "Sasha! The bag!" I yelled.

I held out my arm for Sasha to take the
tote bag hanging from the crook of my elbow and
dared to open my eyes again, but the witch had lost

interest in me. Instead, she had Sasha pinned with her fiery glare.

"Close your eyes, Sasha, don't let her look into your *eyes!*" I screamed, my voice cracking as I slowly regained my strength, but Sasha didn't seem to be able to hear me. She sat slumped on the ground.

I'd no time to waste; my very fears were playing out in front of me. *I had to stop her.* I dug deep in the bag and grabbed a handful of the coarse salt, Grandpops's tale reverberating in my mind.

"So gather your salt, from di glow of the bay.
Gather your salt and mek haste, no delay.
Gather it up so you can dash it down,
at her feet, on her skin, till she bun to di ground."

"I've already lost Grandpops, I *won't* lose Ramone and Sasha too!" I cried out, throwing the salt with all my might.

The witch shrieked, recoiling as crimson smoke rose off her skin. She turned abruptly to face me, lunging forwards, but I dodged her, throwing more.

She shrank away, shielding herself with her mangled hands, her form changing before my eyes – a blur of shapes and colours, until all that was left was an old frame, thin and ailing; her once blazing eyes now a flickering flame, as the smoke danced around her, red wisps snaking high into the air.

It was working.

I didn't stop. I threw fistful after fistful; my fear, my anger, my sadness, my confusion, until there was nothing left. The tote bag fell on the ground, thin and hollow, in front of a smouldering pile of ash, which was all that was left of the Ember Witch. I looked over to see Sasha standing up rubbing her eyes like she'd just been shaken out of a nap.

"Cianne?" she called weakly, looking confused.

I grabbed her, holding on tight, as she squeezed me back. "Thank goodness you're OK," I breathed, tears pricking my eyes.

What about Ramone?

I swallowed the painful lump rising in my throat, hoping I'd done enough to save him. *Please. Please be all right,* I pleaded as I faced the house, clutching Sasha's hand.

I held my breath as the porch door flew open, my heart bursting in my chest. It had never been so good to see the sight of my brother standing there; his big, bright smile telling me he was happy to see me too.

We ran to him and he hugged us both, his eyes shining with tears as he pulled away. "You did it!" he said. "I should have *trusted* you. Grandpops would've been so proud. And even though I'm angry with you for doing something so *dangerous* – " He prodded me. "I'm proud of you too."

A warmth spread from my chest making my scalp tingle. *I did it.* And even though we didn't have Grandpops, we have our memories of him, and those memories kept us safe, just like he promised.

Book talk questions

Do you know any traditional tales from other parts of the world?

Who do you most identify with in the book?

Would you have done anything differently to the characters?

What do Cianne, Sasha and Ramone each contribute to defeating the Ember Witch?

What is Grandpops's importance to the story?

What skills were most useful in defeating the Ember Witch?

Did you find any parts of the book scary?

What do you think Grandpops would have thought about how the children behaved?

Do you know any other stories about shapeshifters?

Who was your favourite character in the book?

Ask the author

What do you enjoy about writing?

I really enjoy expressing my thoughts and feelings through writing. I love being able to let my imagination run free and being creative with ideas – it feels exciting when it all starts to come together on a page.

Tarnelia Matthews

What inspired you to retell the Caribbean folk tale of the Ember Witch?

I heard lots of interesting Caribbean folk tales growing up but I realised I hadn't heard much of the *Ember Witch* and thought it could be an interesting story to retell.

Do you have a favourite place to write?

I find I'm able to write in many spaces, but I do require quiet to do so – and a good cup of tea and some snacks to keep me going.

What drew you to the idea of a shapeshifter?

A shapeshifter presents an element of surprise and mystery – you don't always know what to expect. I wanted to bring those elements of mystery and intrigue to the reader.

What aspects of Caribbean culture did you want to highlight in this retelling?

I really wanted to highlight Caribbean folklore and the many stories that have been passed down through generations, most of which originated from African Mythology. Caribbean folklore is a rich tapestry that also incorporates elements from indigenous and Caribbean Asian cultures. I too wanted to honour the cultural tradition of storytelling by presenting my own.

How did you create suspense and fear?

By not giving the plot away too soon! I created characters that were curious and uncertain. Sometimes sitting in the unknown can create a sense of suspense and fear for readers, especially when adding spooky occurrences!

What do you hope readers take away from the story?

I'd like readers to remain open–minded and remember that there can be much to learn from the old stories that our wise elders have told us.

Collins
BIG CAT

Published by Collins
An imprint of HarperCollins*Publishers*

The News Building   Macken House
1 London Bridge Street   39/40 Mayor Street Upper
London SE1 9GF   Dublin 1
UK   D01 C9W8
                          Ireland

Text © Tarnelia Matthews 2025
Design and illustrations © HarperCollins*Publishers* Limited 2025

10 9 8 7 6 5 4 3 2 1

ISBN 978-0-00-874491-5

British Library Cataloguing-in-Publication Data
A catalogue record for this publication is available from the British Library.

Author: Tarnelia Matthews
Illustrator: Rachel Moss
Publisher: Laura White
Commissioning editor: Holly Woolnough
Development editor: Zoë Clarke
Product manager: Holly Woolnough
Content editor: Selin Akca
Copyeditor: Sally Byford
Proofreader: Catherine Dakin
Reviewer: Lisa Davis
Cover designer: Sarah Finan
Internal design: 2Hoots Publishing Services Ltd
Typesetter: Jouve India Ltd
Production controller: Katharine Willard

Collins would like to thank the teachers and children at Grange Primary School, Southwark, for being
part of the development of Big Cat Read On.

Printed in the UK

Get the latest Collins Big Cat news at
collins.co.uk/collinsbigcat